LITTLE FOX'S SECRET

THE MYSTERY OF BENT'S FORT

Publisher's Cataloging-in-Publication
(Provided by Quality Books, Inc.)

Finley, Mary Peace.
    Little Fox's secret : the mystery of Bent's
Fort / by Mary Peace Finley ; illustrated by
Martha Jane Spurlock. -- 1st ed.
    p.cm.
    SUMMARY: After Cheyenne leader Gray Owl has a
vision of eleven-year-old Little Fox involved in
the destruction of Bent's Fort trading post in
1849, the boy is taken there to play his role
and to learn why it is necessary.
    LCCN: 98-83091
    ISBN: 0-86541-050-X

    1. Bent's Fort (Colo.)--Juvenile fiction.
    2. Cheyenne Indians--Colorado--Juvenile fiction.
    3. Cholera--Colorado--Juvenile fiction.
    I. Spurlock, Martha Jane. II. Title.

PZ7.F4962Li 1999   [Fic]
                    QB199-153

Filter Press, LLC
P.O. Box 95
Palmer Lake, Colorado 80133

Manufactured in the United States of America

Author web site: www.marypeacefinley.com

LITTLE FOX'S SECRET

THE MYSTERY OF BENT'S FORT

MARY PEACE FINLEY

Illustrated by
Martha Jane Spurlock

FILTER PRESS, LLC
Palmer Lake, Colorado

To Wally

beloved companion, husband, best friend

With appreciation to all the rangers, staff,

and volunteers at

Bent's Old Fort National Historic Site.

M.P.F.

Chapter 1
The Season to Trade

Little Fox leapt over the familiar pile of fallen logs—two logs higher today. Arms raised high, he plunged into the stream, scrambled up the crumbling bank, and raced along the worn path into the clearing. The spear at the end of the course came into view. His moccasins pounded dust. His lungs burned. He jerked the spear from the soft prairie soil. "Aaaaiii!" he cried, thrusting the spear above his head. "Hiiii!"

Panting, he sank down onto the stump of a tree. "Faster. Faster than last time." The other young braves were still far behind.

Little Fox imagined his next victory. *Even without the machine to count time, I know this season when we go to trade at Bent's Fort, I will run faster than Robert Bent. My arrow will shoot farther, and it will shoot straighter. This time, Robert will not pin me to the ground when we wrestle.* "No, my friend. I have been practicing. You beat me in my ninth summer, and you won again last year, but you will not beat me this time."

When his breathing returned to normal, Little Fox loped back into the Cheyenne village. The feather adornments on the spear fluttered at his side.

"Who won today?" Painted Horse called out from beside his tipi, the way he did every day.

"I did!" Little Fox answered, the way he did every day. Knowing Painted Horse could not hear, he stomped his foot hard and hit his chest with his fist.

"Yes! Yes! I hear you." Painted Horse touched his finger tips to his ears. "I feel the pounding of your feet. My young friend of eleven summers, you are a clever Little Fox...and a fast one, too. Because of you, we will eat well today."

Little Fox circled Painted Horse's tipi, then circled his own. His sister, Morning Flower, was adding hot stones to the stew cooking inside a buffalo paunch. His mother was roasting the grouse

Little Fox had shot with his bow and arrow early that morning. The grouse were skewered on a green willow stick that rested in the forks of two branches stuck into the ground. The juices dripped and sizzled on the coals and made Little Fox's mouth water.

"When we go to trade at Bent's Fort, Robert will be surprised," Little Fox said, kneeling beside the fire. "Morning Flower, will you watch me win?"

Morning Flower flipped her long black braids over her shoulder. Her eyes sparkled. "I hope we go soon."

"Gray Owl has called for a gathering tonight." Their mother's eyebrows arched, and Little Fox knew what her words—and that look—could mean.

He glanced around the village. Women were finishing their work. No new hides were being scraped. None of the dogs were carrying more firewood into camp. Nothing new was being started.

"What will Gray Owl say? Do you think we will leave for Bent's Fort tomorrow?" A spot in the side of Little Fox's neck beat faster.

His mother's eyebrows lifted again, and she smiled.

"I'll take my two buffalo robes!" Little Fox said. "I'll trade them for a knife of silver."

"I'll trade my best woven basket for an iron pot. An iron pot won't split like a gourd or dry and burn like the stomach of the buffalo. I will visit Old Grandmother, and see Yellow Woman's and William Bent's new baby." Little Fox could tell his mother was as excited about returning to Bent's Fort as he was.

"It's time to move," Morning Flower said. "We have been in this place since before the last full moon."

"We are a people who move," Little Fox said. "I like to follow the seasons and the buffalo. I like for all the prairie to be my home. I don't have to stay in one place like Robert does when he's with his father at Bent's Fort." But now Little Fox could hardly wait to get back to the two-story adobe trading post again.

Chapter 2
Gray Owl's Vision

Excitement hung over the village that night as everyone gathered around a large, roaring fire. Gray Owl was seated cross-legged on a buffalo robe. The flames from the fire flicked shadows on the deep crags in his brown leathery face. Five of his most honored braves stood beside him. When everyone was in place, it was one of the braves, not Gray Owl, who spoke.

"I speak for Gray Owl," said the brave. "Gray Owl has been given a vision."

Whispers stirred around the circle.

"This is the season when we travel southeast," the brave continued, "to the Fort of our brother, William Bent, to trade."

"I will trade for a knife with a silver blade." Little Fox made the sign of a knife to his group of friends.

"I will trade for sweet candy and coffee beans that make the black soup...."

"...glass beads and needles from England..."

"...steel for making fire..."

The brave raised his voice and the murmuring stilled. "Gray Owl has seen a vision." The fire crackled, and Little Fox leaned forward, waiting to

hear. "The Cheyenne will not go to Bent's Fort this year."

Will not go!

Silence hovered over the gathered tribe.

"Soldiers wearing blue uniforms have come from the United States. White men have fouled water holes. They have slaughtered many buffalo and left the meat to rot. They have brought sickness and death. The sickness is spreading among the tribes of the plains. We will not go."

"But William Bent is one of us! He is not a soldier from the United States. Bent's Fort is a trading post, not a military post!" A young brave protested. "His first wife was Owl Woman and his second wife is Yellow Woman, her sister. His children's grandmother is the grandmother of our children. We are family."

A great commotion broke out. Little Fox grasped at phrases and words that sped by him, struggling to understand. His people had always gone to Bent's Fort. The great adobe trading post was a wonderful place filled with wondrous things.

Gray Owl lifted his great warbonnet to his head and slowly rose to his feet. His white-coated eyes looked blindly over the people. Argument stopped. Little Fox shivered. *Why a warbonnet?* The fire crackled, sending a shower of sparks high into the air. The sparks flared, then one by one, died.

Finally Gray Owl spoke.

"There is a great evil at the white man's trading post." His voice was hoarse. "Death has come to the Fort of our brother. Now the Fort belongs to death. Never again will the Cheyenne trade at William Bent's mighty Fort. This I have seen."

Little Fox sank to the ground. Would he never race Robert again? Would he never trade his buffalo robes for a knife with a blade of silver? He could barely listen as Gray Owl continued.

"Tomorrow, I alone go to Bent's Fort to tell our brother, William Bent, what I have seen. I will warn him of what is to come. Only these five braves will accompany me. These five—" Gray Owl's finger pointed one by one, down the line of men his blind eyes could not see "—and one more." His head pivoted slowly as if he were listening, then stopped, facing Little Fox. "Little Fox. You, too, will go."

Chapter 3
Frijol

Even his mother treated Little Fox differently this morning, but he could not answer her question. He could not answer anyone's question. He could not answer his own. *Why me?*

Now his friends stared wide-eyed at the brave who had spoken for Gray Owl the night before. He had come for Little Fox.

"Come with me, Little Fox. You must have a pony."

Little Fox leaned toward Morning Flower. "Help mother, Morning Flower," Little Fox said softly. "Use your bow and arrow to shoot rabbits, quail, grouse. Enough for Painted Horse, too."

Morning Flower's wide eyes looked solemn, scared.

"You can do it, Morning Flower," he whispered. "You have to."

Little Fox followed the brave away from the cluster of tipis. The ponies were of every color—black, silver, red-brown—small, alert ponies whose eager eyes turned toward him. Their nostrils flared, taking in his scent, and their ears leaned forward.

"Which one?" Little Fox asked.

"Gray Owl said you could choose any pony you want."

Little Fox looked for a long time before he chose the pony with red marks on white. "Your red spots shine in the sun. You are as speckled as the Mexican beans we trade for," Little Fox said, rubbing the horse's soft muzzle with the palm of his hand. "I will call you Frijol."

Frijol ducked his head and blew into Little Fox's face, and Little Fox knew he had made two right choices—the right pony and the right name.

He led Frijol to his tipi. His mother stood outside holding his buffalo robes, a leather bag filled with pemmican and jerky for him to eat, and another bag of provisions. His bow and arrows and her woven basket to trade for an iron pot sat on the grass beside her.

As soon as the provisions were strapped on Frijol, Little Fox mounted. Only once did he look back. His mother, Morning Flower, Painted Horse, and his friends stood motionless, telling him good-bye only with their eyes.

Little Fox rode to the edge of camp and fell in behind Gray Owl and the five braves, last in line. Gray Owl's voice reached back to him. "Little Fox,

ride in front. Beside me." That was the place of honor. *Why? Why me?*

Early morning mist rose from the river. Blackbirds trilled. Geese rose from a calm backwater, stretching their long necks and honking, making Little Fox's fingers yearn for his bow. Behind him, the lodge poles of the tipis and the smoke from morning fires slid farther and farther from sight.

Ahead, the sun glared up from the edge of the world. Bright rays shone on Gray Owl's face and on the wrinkled lids of his closed eyes. "Why me, Gray Owl?"

Without turning his head, Gray Owl answered. "It is as I have seen."

"But what have you seen, Gray Owl? Why am *I* going?"

Gray Owl's ash-colored pony snorted and shook his head. Gray Owl said nothing.

Their pace was steady and slow. Sometimes during the next three days, the five braves behind them laughed and joked, but Gray Owl did not talk, and he did not laugh.

"Why me, Frijol?" Little Fox asked, so softly Gray Owl wouldn't hear. "Is it because Robert is my friend? Is it because I run fast? Or because I am so small? What will I have to do?"

Frijol's ears swiveled and twitched, and Little

Fox was sure that if Frijol knew, he would tell. Their breath and their thoughts had become the same, and Little Fox imagined that they had become one—part boy, part pony, one new kind of creature.

Late in the evening of the third day, Gray Owl, the five braves, and Little Fox rode down from the sunset on the sloping flat-topped high plain, across a row of steep sand hills, and into the valley of the river the white men named "Arkansas." Billowy green cottonwoods lined the river banks, but the valley floor looked trampled and worn. Prairie grasses were short-cropped and brown. Ruts and paths converged like lines in a spider web at the huge double gates of Bent's Fort.

Above the belfry a red, white and blue flag waved—the flag of the Americans. "Look, Frijol. Bent's Fort!" Little Fox whispered. "The Fort is even bigger than I remembered. It looks like a mountain butte against the setting sun."

Even from this distance, Little Fox could hear the ring of the blacksmith's anvil and the shouts of men and the screech of giant birds with fanning blue feathers that Robert called "peacocks." There was no cloud in the sky, but a cold shadow shivered across Little Fox's shoulders. *What will happen down there? What will I have to do?* He raised up higher on Frijol's back, trying to see Robert.

"Look well," Gray Owl said, twisting on his saddle blanket to face the five braves. "You will not see this Fort again."

"Not see the Fort again!" Little Fox dared to speak. "Gray Owl. You are blind. How can you know what we see?"

"My vision comes from the world of spirit," Gray Owl answered, but for Little Fox, the answer was a mystery.

Chapter 4
The Warning

Every other time they had come to Bent's Fort, the tribe had pitched camp outside the Fort's walls before they went inside. But this time, Gray Owl and Little Fox, followed by the five braves, rode directly toward the great metal-clad wooden gates. The ponies' hooves beat a solemn steady rhythm, like the slow beat of a drum. Outside, they dismounted, but the beat seemed to continue as they walked through the dark, cool passageway into the courtyard.

Gray Owl stood, arms crossed, waiting. Little Fox glanced at him, folded his own arms, and tried to see everything around him without moving his eyes. His stomach growled at the scent of roasting meat and boiling coffee.

"Gray Owl!" William Bent emerged from a room on the second floor catwalk. "Welcome!" His feet scraped down the open stairs that led into the courtyard. By the giant fur press stacked with buffalo pelts, he stopped.

Gray Owl had not spoken, and Little Fox could see that William Bent sensed something wrong. William Bent's eyes glanced to the side and gave Little Fox a look of recognition.

To his right, on the second floor, Little Fox heard coughing. Several American soldiers wearing blue pants and no shirts were sprawled against the adobe walls in the last rays of sun.

"Gray Owl," William Bent finally spoke. "I did not know you were coming. You did not send word. Where are the others?"

"The others will not come." Gray Owl said. "I myself bring word. Where is your wife, Yellow Woman, and Old Grandmother?"

"They and the children have gone to the Tribal Council with the Kiowa and Osage and others," Bent answered, but his voice was guarded. "Gray Owl, what is wrong? We are family. You can speak freely."

Gray Owl's chest rose. Little Fox could hear the air moving in, then out again. "These soldiers..." Gray Owl gestured upward without turning his head. "Your trading post is destroying us, William Bent. Now Bent's Fort shall be destroyed. This, I have seen."

Destroyed! Little Fox jerked.

William Bent's dark eyes flared. Furrows sunk more deeply into his pox-marked face. His breathing became shallow.

On the second floor catwalk, the giant blue-feathered bird screeched and fanned its tail. Little Fox glanced up, and there stood Robert. Their eyes met, but Little Fox did not know what his eyes should say.

"I have received the vision," Gray Owl said. "You have been warned." Then he turned and Little Fox turned with him. Gray Owl and Little Fox, followed by the five braves, walked back through the dark, cool passageway out of the Fort.

Chapter 5
Small Warrior

"Will we leave, now that William Bent has been warned?" Little Fox leaned forward to speak softly into Frijol's ear. "Gray Owl told what he has seen."

Frijol shook his mane and pawed at the dusty ground.

What Gray Owl had seen in the vision was worse than Little Fox imagined. Before, Gray Owl had not said the Fort would be destroyed. Little Fox stared over his shoulder. *Nothing that big can be destroyed!*

Frijol kept an even pace with Gray Owl's pony, even when Gray Owl turned the opposite way from what Little Fox expected. Little Fox looked back at the five braves, then studied Gray Owl's face. *Maybe vision from the spirit world happens only at special times. Maybe Gray Owl doesn't know he has turned toward the river instead of back toward our village. Maybe he has brought me to be his eyes.* "Gray Owl..." Little Fox started to speak.

Gray Owl answered before Little Fox said any more. "We will stop by the river."

They stopped. The five braves caught fish from the river to cook over a small fire. Even they were quiet now. As night began to fall, there was no laughter. No joking. First one, then another, turned to look at the Fort. Then they looked at Little Fox. *They feel it, too,* Little Fox thought. *They know something is about to happen.*

"Little Fox! Come!" Gray Owl's words crackled through the darkness like sparks from the fire.

Little Fox sprang boldly to his feet to hide the trembling he felt inside. He stepped toward Gray Owl who sat cross-legged and motionless with his back to the flames, facing the great adobe walls of the white man's trading post. He could not see Gray Owl's white-coated eyes, but he felt those old eyes peering deep inside him, searching for something.

Little Fox clenched and unclenched his toes, digging ridges in the dirt beneath his moccasins, waiting for Gray Owl to speak. Behind him, the five Cheyenne braves sat in silence, also waiting.

Abruptly, Gray Owl leaned forward. The rush of his power swept over Little Fox with the force of a mighty wind. Fingers of cold brushed across his neck.

"Little brave of eleven summers—" Gray Owl's voice rasped of dry reeds. "Now you will know why I have brought you to this place." He tilted his head back, his face toward the dark sky. "I have seen this Fort crumbling into dust. Destroyed!" His hands swooped up high into the air, then leveled.

One gnarled finger pointed straight into Little Fox's chest. "And I have seen that it is you, small warrior, who destroys it."

Little Fox's knees buckled. Shaking, he lowered himself onto the ground. Smoke from the fire spiraled upward. Little Fox tasted ash on his tongue. Behind him, a rumble of astonished voices rose like the roar of a mountain waterfall. Then Gray Owl stood. Suddenly the five braves were moving around him, swinging themselves onto their mounts. Little Fox's buffalo pelts and bags of provisions landed on the ground, stirring dust. "We will return for you, Little Fox," Gray Owl said, "when it is done."

Little Fox scrambled to his feet, grabbing the coarse mane of Gray Owl's pony. "But how? How, Gray Owl? The Fort is like a mountain. How can I destroy it?"

"The vision has shown only that you will. It has not shown how." Gray Owl turned his pony, then paused. His voice rasped, "You must be clever like your name. You must become a little fox."

Gray Owl and the five braves circled, then rode away. "Frijol!" Little Fox cried. "Not you, too!" His voice dropped to a whisper. "Gray Owl! Can't you leave Frijol...here...with me?"

Little Fox stared out into the darkness, his ears straining after each retreating step of the ponies' hooves. Soon the only sounds that remained were the gentle swish of the lazy river and clacking of leaves as the night breeze stirred through the cottonwoods.

Slowly, he turned toward the massive black shape of the fort. *How?* The question hung like smoke through the long, long night. *How? How can I become a fox? How can I destroy Bent's Fort?*

Chapter 6
A Friend and An Enemy

In the early morning twilight, the Fort loomed even larger than it had in the darkness of night. Little Fox saw the black barrel of a cannon on the round tower nearest him. A few men were walking and riding outside the gates. Some of them were soldiers dressed in blue.

No one would be surprised by a Cheyenne camp near the Fort. They would be surprised, though, Little Fox thought, by a Cheyenne camp of one—one eleven-year-old boy who has not yet sought a vision; not yet become a man. He would build a shelter in the trees that bordered the river. Even if no one knew why he was there, it would be better to stay out of sight—like a fox.

Little Fox gathered long, narrow branches lying on the ground and hanging low from the trees, then stacked them in a pile next to an old, whitened cottonwood. The tree was only half-alive, hollow at the base and in the middle, but most of its trunk was solid.

He scraped dried bark and dead leaves from inside the hole in the tree trunk to make a place to store his bag of provisions. Then one after another, he propped the tips of the long limbs in the V of the cottonwood where the branches met. He leaned the limbs in a semicircle three layers deep around the tree trunk, angling them outward to make enough room to curl up inside. At the top, it stood taller than he was. He slid one of the buffalo pelts over the frame. It was a wickiup, not as good as a tipi, but a shelter. At least for now, a home to protect him from rain and wind.

Little Fox bathed in the river, then ate some of the pemmican from his leather bag, wondering what he should do next. He remembered Gray Owl's other visions. When their tribe had been hungry, Gray Owl had "seen" the buffalo in a vision of the plains near the salty springs. The hunters went, and the buffalo were there. Gray Owl had "seen" the injured woman by the river, and the braves had found her just where he said they would. Many tales of the tribe told of battles fought and won because of Gray Owl's visions.

But why am I the one? I'm not yet a warrior. I have only a small bag of flints at my waist, and my bow and arrows. I don't have a gun, or even a good knife. And I don't want to hurt Robert or his father. They're my friends. But Gray Owl saw....

Gray Owl saw.

So it would be true. Little Fox imagined his return to the tribe, an honored hero. His mother and Morning Flower would smile. Painted Horse would say, "Yes! Yes! I hear you," the way he always did. Little Fox didn't know how, but what Gray Owl saw would happen. It always did.

First, he must learn all he could about the Fort. To get inside again, he would trade the other buffalo robe for a knife with a silver blade and he would trade his mother's basket for an iron pot. As much as he wanted to, he would not say he had come to race with Robert. "I can't be a friend and an enemy at the same time. I can't! I won't! I'll stay away from Robert!" he said aloud.

Gray Owl's words echoed in his memory, "You must be clever like your name," and he wondered. Did he appear in Gray Owl's vision *because* he was Robert's friend?

He put his mother's basket on top of the buffalo robe and slid his hands and arms beneath the bundle. Boldly, he strode from the shelter of the trees onto the open prairie and toward the Fort.

A white man with a face splotched red like Frijol's coat leaned over one of the Fort's round towers and waved. His hair was the color of pumpkin. Little Fox couldn't understand his words, so he lifted the robe and basket to show he wanted to trade.

The metal-clad gates swung open, and the man with the pumpkin hair led Little Fox into the dark entryway. It was like a trap, closing, and Little

Fox wanted to bolt and run. But the entry opened
into the large sunlit courtyard, and Little Fox
breathed again. He'd been here yesterday and many
times before, but now he stared around him at the
wooden fur press, the second layer of rooms and
catwalks, and at the thick mud walls, seeing them
as something new—something to be destroyed. His
hand edged from under the buffalo robe and
touched the adobe. It was like stone. *How can
I break stone?*

"Come on in here if you want to trade that robe." The white man with the orange hair pointed to one of the doors on the ground floor.

Little Fox guessed the meaning of the words and followed him inside. What he saw made a sound of surprise escape from his lips. His hand covered his mouth. Rows of shelves were stacked with striped blankets, jars of candy, bolts of fabric, colored metal boxes, candles, and beads. Ropes, beaver traps, twists of tobacco, and leather harnesses hung from the ceiling. Polished barrels of long rifles leaned against the wall. The trade room had more things than he'd ever seen in one place, and things he'd never seen before. His fingers wanted to reach out and touch each one, but he held his hands close.

The pumpkin-haired American laughed. "Well?"

First Little Fox placed the basket in front of him and pointed to a large iron kettle. The American turned the basket over and over in his hands, making appreciative sounds. He set the iron kettle on the wooden counter with a loud thump. "It's a trade," he said. "What else do you have there?"

Then Little Fox slid the folded buffalo robe onto the counter while his eyes searched the shelves. Spotting the knives, he pointed. The American frowned. He lifted a bag of candy. Little Fox refused to look at it. The American pointed to a coil of rope.

27

Again Little Fox refused to look. The American laughed again, then said something as he handed Little Fox a knife with a silver blade.

"He says he hopes you won't take this on the warpath."

Little Fox spun around to see who had spoken the Cheyenne words.

"Robert!"

Chapter 7
The Munitions Room

"Why are you here alone?" Robert asked, motioning Little Fox to follow him out into the courtyard.

Little Fox slipped his new knife into the leather bag at his side and grasped the metal handle of the cast iron pot. "I—I came to trade."

"But why alone?" Robert insisted. Robert had grown since Little Fox had last seen him. He was taller now. His dark hair was longer than it had been before. His pants were not made of leather. His white shirt was woven from American cloth. Robert leaned against a peeled log post under the catwalk. "Where are Gray Owl and the five braves who were with you yesterday?"

"They've gone."

"Where?"

Little Fox thought quickly. "They will come back for me...I have to go now." *I must not have anything to do with Robert,* Little Fox remembered.

"Go! Why?" Robert grabbed at the iron pot. "Are you going to cook a buffalo hump? What's the matter with you, Little Fox? Come on! Let's race." Robert sprang away from the wooden post and sprinted toward the corral at the back of the fort, dodging in and out among the milling travelers, traders, and trappers. "I'll bet your pony isn't as fast as mine! Come on."

"Frijol's not my pony." Reluctantly, Little Fox trailed Robert across the courtyard and into a dark passageway. "Gray Owl took him."

"Took him!" Stopping, Robert laughed. "So where are you going without a pony?"

Little Fox couldn't think of anything to say. He heard coughing and looked up at the second floor catwalk, at the sick American soldiers he'd seen yesterday lying in the sun, and at the rows of dark open doorways. Little Fox remembered Gray Owl's words at the campfire, "They bring the sickness that kills—" Was the sickness here, too? On his left he heard a hammer bouncing against an anvil, the rasp of metal against wood, and a loud whooshing sound.

"Why are you staring at everything, Little Fox?" Robert asked. "Haven't you seen the Fort before?"

"Yes," Little Fox said, peering down another wide passageway cramped with broken wagons. "But only there—" He nodded toward the courtyard, "and the trading room."

"Well, then, come on. I'll show you." It wasn't going to be easy to stay away from Robert. *If I try to leave now*, Little Fox thought, *Robert will stop me.*

Or follow me. I don't want him to know where I built my wickiup.

"—but our caravan came back before we reached St. Louis," Robert was saying. "Many people are dying of a terrible sickness in the white settlements. My father brought me back here to keep me away from it."

"Are you away from it? Those soldiers—" Little Fox nodded toward the sick men above them.

Robert looked down at the brown American shoes on his feet. "I don't know," he answered, and for awhile, he was quiet. Robert led Little Fox along the front of the workshops into a cool, large room with a long table. "Anyway, I'm glad you're here. With my brother and sister at the Tribal Council, there's nothing much to do."

The room joined a huge indoor kitchen where a woman was cooking. She laughed at Robert, and handed both Robert and Little Fox sweet bread to eat. The sweet taste made little streams flood the insides of Little Fox's mouth. He was still licking the sparkles of sugar from his fingers as he followed Robert into the room with the whooshing sound. The blacksmith grumbled something at them and tugged at the rope on a large bellows that hung from the ceiling. Air rushed into the glowing coals that flared hot on Little Fox's skin. "Look in there. That's the carpenter shop." Robert jabbed Little Fox

31

with his elbow and pointed to the room next door.

What a place of wonders! Little Fox ducked into a room with wood of every kind and patterns and wheels and tools made of metal.

The carpenter winked at him and said, "Want to give it a try?" He held out a long piece of metal with jagged see-saw teeth. Little Fox's fingers fit into the wooden handle, and the long blade quivered and sang as it touched wood. Little Fox pulled. The saw teeth raked through a board, and he laughed.

He almost forgot why he was there.

"Come on!" Robert said. "Let's get some horses and chase the buffalo in the corral." They ran out of the carpenter's shop past a room that sat alone near a dark corridor. It didn't have windows like the other rooms, and the door was fastened with a long, wooden bolt.

"What's this?" Little Fox paused. The room was a separate little house with its own separate roof.

"The munitions room. It's where we keep the gunpowder and cannon balls."

Gunpowder?

Gunpowder!

Suddenly, Little Fox's question was answered. There *was* a way. The vision Gray Owl had been given *was* possible. Gunpowder could blow up anything, even walls like stone.

Chapter 8
Cholera

Every day for the next three days, Little Fox went to the Fort. He played the Cheyenne hoop game with Robert, and they raced on foot. He won once. Robert, wearing his American shoes, won once. Next they would race the long race, and both would wear moccasins.

Little Fox moved freely in and out of the Fort. He saw William Bent working and trading. Sometimes Bent argued with the men in blue uniforms. Sometimes he took care of them. He always looked worried. Little Fox realized that the Cheyenne called William Bent "Little White Man," only because of his small size, not from any lack of power.

"Little Fox?" William Bent helped Robert hoist a stack of pelts from the press. "Who is helping your mother while you are gone?"

"My sister, Morning Flower."

"Morning Flower is so young!"

"She is in her ninth summer. She can fish, hunt. She is strong." He hoped William Bent would not ask any more questions. It was hard to think about home. Even if Morning Flower was strong, he didn't like her doing all his work and her own work, too.

"Why did Gray Owl leave you here, Little Fox?" William Bent asked, frowning.

"He— I—" Little Fox stammered.

"Old Gray Owl!" Robert brushed dust from his hands. "He's crazy, that's why! He sees what isn't, and doesn't see what is! Huh! We all heard what he said!" Robert hunched his shoulders, squinted his eyes nearly closed, and in a strange, hoarse voice said, "This Fort will be destroyed!" He sounded just like Gray Owl. "This I have seen!"

Little Fox laughed.

"Gray Owl forgot Little Fox, that's what I think." Robert said, sounding like himself again. "Just rode off and forgot him! He'll earn a new name soon—Crazy Owl!"

"But didn't Gray Owl tell you when he would be back?" William Bent peered intently into Little Fox's eyes.

"No," Little Fox answered and looked away. He wanted to run to his wickiup to hide from these questions. He didn't like laughing at Gray Owl. But what if there really was something wrong with Gray Owl's mind?

"Where do you sleep?"

When Little Fox didn't answer William Bent sighed heavily. "Look, Little Fox, there's no reason for you to be out there somewhere all alone. Bring your things in here. If Gray Owl doesn't return soon, I'll send someone out to find him. Or we'll get you back to your village. It's too bad. Gray Owl has been a great man for a very long time...." William Bent walked away shaking his head.

Alone at his campfire in the evening, dark thoughts rumbled through Little Fox's head. He thought about the room with gunpowder. And he thought about Robert and William Bent and how much he liked them. Robert, too, tried to get him to sleep in the Fort, but he refused.

Maybe Robert was right about Gray Owl. Maybe he was crazy. Maybe this time, Gray Owl's vision was only a bad dream. Maybe he had eaten bad food. Maybe the people heard only *some* of Gray Owl's visions of the past—the ones that came true.

Destroy Bent's Fort? Even with gunpowder, it wasn't possible. Destroying the Bents' friendship was.

Outside the Fort gate the next morning the pumpkin-haired American drew a line in the dirt. He held a round timepiece in his hand.

Little Fox and Robert nudged the toes of their moccasins against the line. They would race east along the Santa Fe Trail for two miles to the pile of bleached bones, swim the Arkansas River, race up the opposite bank, swim back across the river, and end here at the gate. Little Fox's heart was already pumping hard, wild with anticipation. *This year I will win!*

"Ready?" the American yelled. "Set?"

"No!" Robert cried. "Look!"

Little Fox stumbled forward. His breath rushed out.

"There's Yellow Woman!" Robert pointed toward a woman leading a horse carrying two children and pulling a travois. They were following the Santa Fe Trail from the east. "And my sister and brother, Mary and George!" Just as Robert began to run toward them, his father dashed from the Fort.

"Yellow Woman!" William Bent called in Cheyenne. "What's wrong? Where is Old Grandmother? Where are the others?"

Little Fox could tell from the looks on the faces of the woman and children that something terrible had happened.

Yellow Woman slumped against her husband, almost too tired to talk. "Old Grandmother died—two days ago. Many are dead—Cheyenne, Kiowa, Osage—"

"It was supposed to be a peaceful tribal council!" William Bent clenched his fists. "Not a battle! I would never have—"

"There was no battle." Robert's brother, George, slid down from the horse. "A Kiowa warrior fell over, like this—" George clutched his stomach. "—and he died. Then another—and then more. And more. And more. People were running everywhere, trying to escape the sickness."

William Bent's face turned gray. "Cholera! It has spread to the tribes."

Then Gray Owl's vision is true!

In the travois a baby began to cry.

"We ran away from it, Father," Mary said, her eyes pleading. "The big cramps, they won't find us here, will they?"

"I hope not, Mary." William Bent stroked Mary's shiny black hair, but there was worry on his face. "I hope not."

Yellow Woman's glazed eyes came to rest on Little Fox, and slowly focused. "Little Fox? Is that you, Little Fox?"

Little Fox nodded.

Yellow Woman's breath rushed in. Her eyes stretched wide. "What are you doing here? Your mother? Morning Flower? Are they dead, too?"

"No, Yellow Woman. They are well."

Little Fox watched William Bent lead the horses and his family into the Fort, then close the gates behind them. The sadness of the Bent family made Little Fox sad, too. And he was sad for Old Grandmother. She was gone. He would never see her again. And he was sorry that he and Robert had not raced. Maybe tomorrow.

Slowly, he walked back to his wickiup in the trees. *Cholera*, William Bent called the sickness. Gray Owl's vision was true, after all. If it would keep the sickness away, the Fort should be destroyed! But Robert and Mary and Charles and Yellow Woman were Cheyenne, like him. They were family. And they were his friends. Even if he could destroy the fort, it would not be right to make their lives even sadder.

Chapter 9
Wait and Watch

Thoughts of the race filled Little Fox's mind as he scrambled out of his bed of leaves in the old cottonwood tree. He had decided. Gray Owl's vision must have been wrong. Or he was mistaken. The vision was only a bad dream. It could not be that Cheyenne would turn against Cheyenne. It could not be that a boy of eleven winters would destroy the Fort and betray William Bent and Yellow Woman and their family.

"I will not think like a fox any more!" Little Fox yelped and jumped into the river to bathe. For the first time in days, he felt like a boy again, not a man in a boy's body. Not like a boy with a man's problem.

He shook the water from his hair, dressed, and ran through the grove of trees toward the Fort. "Watch out, Robert Bent," he said, "This race is mine!" But he stopped short where the trees ended, and backed warily under cover.

Both Fort gates were open wide. Out rolled a heavily loaded wagon carrying Yellow Woman, Mary, and the baby. After that wagon came another, then another, each pulled by a yoke of oxen. Some wagons carried sick soldiers.

Little Fox stared. No wagon train had arrived. No one but Yellow Woman and her stepchildren had come to the Fort. Why was everyone leaving?

By the time the sun stood overhead, as many wagons as Little Fox had fingers—and that many more—had rolled out through the double gates. Robert rode a pony at the very end, pulling a

travois. Turning backwards, he looked toward the grove of cottonwoods. *Looking for me? Should I run out and signal to him? Should I go with him?* But Little Fox crouched low. Cautious. Wary. More like a fox than ever before. *I will wait and watch.* The last wagon churned eastward along the river until the wagons and Robert disappeared in a cloud of dust.

A cold finger brushed Little Fox's neck. "Gray Owl!" Little Fox spun around, but no one was there. No one was in the Fort. Everyone had gone.

The Fort was never left empty, never left unguarded. Never! But today it was, and he was the only one who knew.

This was the time! Gray Owl's vision....

Little Fox grabbed his leather bag, tucked his knife into his waist band and darted toward the Fort. The double gates still hung open. He flattened himself against the cool adobe inside the doorway. The passage was dark, the adobe, rough and cold under his hands. At the opening to the courtyard, he crouched and listened, but the only sounds he heard were the slapping rope on the flag pole and the clucking of a forgotten chicken. A sparrow chirped and hopped across the dirt toward him pecking at bits of nothing.

No one was left. No one would be hurt.

Fingering the sharp flints he would use to start

the fire, Little Fox darted across the courtyard to the munitions room where the gunpowder was stored. Then he skidded to a stop and moaned. The wooden bolt across the door had been fastened with a large metal lock.

Little Fox tugged, but the lock would not budge. He pushed, but the bolt would not slide. He tossed the flints on the ground beside the door. Quickly, he unsheathed his knife and stabbed the wood. The sharp point gouged. Chips flew. The muscles in his arm burned, but he kept hacking around the bolt. He was so intent at his task that he didn't hear the galloping hooves until they were already inside the courtyard.

"Whoa!" someone yelled.

Little Fox jumped. The knife slipped from his fingers as he dived into the shadows.

Grumbling, the rider strode directly toward the munitions room. "What in tarnation?" Little Fox heard his knife being scraped up from the dirt, and he recognized William Bent's voice.

Little Fox huddled against the cold wall, motionless. What would Robert's father do if he found him?

"Who's in here?" Bent roared.

Little Fox could guess what those words meant, but he didn't answer.

"Come on out!" Bent was getting closer.

Little Fox backed through the shadowy passageway toward the round room where he'd seen saddles stored. From there he could escape up the ladder to the northwest tower, or out into the corral. But just as he slipped through the doorway, his foot hit something soft. There was a loud squawk and a flutter of wings as a chicken bustled out of his way. In the next instant, Little Fox felt the iron grip of a hand on his arm, dragging him into the light.

Chapter 10
The Boom That
Shook The Wickiup

"Little Fox!" Bent's face was angry. Sweat beaded his forehead. His eyes looked wild, like an animal's. "You?" He threw back his head and laughed, a crazy howling laugh. Little Fox struggled to get away, but William Bent's fingers dug more deeply into his skin. The knife blade flashed.

Bent switched from English to Cheyenne. "So this is why Gray Owl left you here, is it?" He laughed again, a mean laugh. "Did you think you could blow up my Fort, Little Fox? You? With your little knife and flints?" The knife landed on the ground. Bent's eyes narrowed into black holes. "You'd blow yourself up that way, that's all!" He shook his head. His grip on Little Fox loosened. "Enough of your people have already died. Many more will die before this is over. Little Fox, *you* must live!"

Bent reached into his pocket, drew out a small piece of metal and thrust it into a hole in the munitions room lock.

"Open it!" Bent growled.

Little Fox's fingers trembled as he pushed and turned the key. Something inside the metal clicked and the lock sprang open.

Wooden kegs of gunpowder were stacked on their sides against the walls inside. William Bent stabbed a finger toward them. "One spark! One spark, Little Fox, from your flint—one spark from your knife—and BOOM!"

Little Fox jumped.

"You'd be dead. But not the Fort, Little Fox. Not the Fort. Do you understand?" Bent's voice was raspy. He was short of breath.

Little Fox nodded. He couldn't swallow, couldn't talk.

"If you wanted to blow up my Fort, Little Fox, you'd put powder there—and there!—and there!—and there!" Wildly, Bent pointed from one place to another. "You'd take these kegs like this—" He stepped through the munitions room doorway, gently lifted a middle-sized barrel, and carried it out cradled like a baby. "Take one!" he ordered. Sweat trickled down the sides of his face.

Trembling, Little Fox ducked inside and rolled a powder keg into his arms. He followed Bent up the stairs to the room where the soldiers had been.

"You'd make a sling," Bent said, "like this—" He carefully set the keg on the floor, looped a rope three times over the rafter, then gently lifted the barrel. "—and you'd hang a powder keg inside— very—very—carefully. Like this." Breathing heavily, he slipped the barrel into the loops, and let go. The barrel swayed under the wooden beam. "Then you'd hang another one here." He slid a rope over a second log. "And you'd say to the United States government, 'No! I will not sell my Fort to you! It's a trading post, not a military post. It's not a charity hospital for your soldiers. And it will not be used to war against Mexico or the tribes!'" He lifted the second keg from Little Fox's arms. "Or a place to breed cholera!"

Back they went for more and more and more until powder kegs dangled in every room on the second floor. All the while, Robert's father raged. "And then, Little Fox—" Bent glared down a nose that looked like an eagle's beak, and grabbed Little Fox roughly by the arms. "—if you hadn't blown yourself up yet, and if you still wanted to destroy my Fort, you'd take some cannon fuse—" He pulled a coiled white rope from the munitions room. "—and you'd run it from one keg to another—like this!"

He stomped up the stairs, attached the fuse first to one barrel and then to the next until they were strung together like squash on a vine. Then he lowered the rest of the fuse over the edge of the second floor catwalk to the courtyard below.

"And then—" William Bent shouted, even though Little Fox was standing right beside him. "You would get your knife and my horse and—"

Little Fox didn't wait to hear any more. He dashed downstairs, scooped up his flints and knife, grabbed the reins of Bent's horse and ran. Bent unrolled the end of the cannon fuse through the open gates and onto the trampled grass outside. When the last loop lay flat, Bent straightened. Very quietly, he said, "And then, Little Fox, you would promise never to speak of what you have seen today."

Silently, he looked deep into Little Fox's eyes, then he looked back at the Fort. Something caught in his throat—his last words were only a whisper, "And then you'd say good-bye."

Scraping a thin stick that burst into flame, Bent paused only a moment, then touched the flame to the fuse. Hissing like a snake, sparks danced down the white cord toward the Fort.

Bent jerked the reins of his prancing horse from Little Fox's hand. "If you wanted to destroy my Fort, Little Fox," he bellowed, "that's what you'd do!" Mounting, he kicked the horse and galloped away.

Little Fox raced across the plain into the stand of cottonwoods by the river. He dived into his wickiup just as the first muffled explosion shook the ground. Dust and black smoke slowly rose from the Fort. BOOM! BOOM! BOOM! Flames roared upward—BOOM! BOOM!—jarring the wickiup with each new explosion.

The rumble of collapsing walls and the hiss of flames continued into the night.

Early the next morning, Gray Owl, the five braves, and Frijol returned. The braves pointed toward the crumbling ruins that still smoldered in the dawn. They looked at Little Fox with wonder, silently waiting.

Gray Owl stood apart, his old face serene in the light of the rising sun. "Is it as I have seen?"

What can I tell him? That I tried and failed? That William Bent blew up his own Fort? I promised I would not tell.

"Yes, Gray Owl," Little Fox finally answered. "It is as you have seen."

And he said no more.

What Really Happened?
Some Historical Facts

In the mid-1800s the United States extended
no farther west than the Missouri border. From
there, the Santa Fe Trail crossed the territory of the
Plains Tribes to the town of Santa Fe which was
then in Mexico. For a trader traveling by wagon, the
first roof between the American settlements in
Missouri and Santa Fe was six or seven weeks away
at Bent's Fort on the Arkansas River in what is now
southeastern Colorado.

In the early days of Bent's Fort, trappers,
traders, and the people of many tribes—Cheyenne,
Ute, Kiowa, Delaware and others—brought pelts of
beaver and buffalo to Bent's Fort to trade for
American and European equipment and supplies.
Mexican goods passed eastward through the Fort to
sell in the United States. U.S. merchandise was
shipped west and south to market in Mexico whose
border was then the Arkansas River, a stone's
throw from Bent's Fort. It was a time of abundance
and prosperity at Bent's Fort.

William Bent married Owl Woman and became
closely linked with her Cheyenne tribe. After Owl
Woman died in childbirth, William married
Owl Woman's sister, Yellow Woman. Yellow

Woman's niece and nephews became her daughter and sons.

During the Mexican-American War (1846-1848), the United States government took advantage of the Fort's strategic position on the Mexican border. Supplies belonging to William Bent were used, but not paid for. Soldiers, often sick, bunked at the Fort, but the government didn't pay for their care. Bent's business was ruined. The government pressured Bent to sell the Fort for a military post, but Bent would not sell. He did not want his Fort used against Mexico or the tribes.

The discovery of gold in California in 1848 brought a wave of American settlers to the Fort. The settlers also brought further destruction to the great plains and to their earlier inhabitants, the Plains Indians. Settlers didn't understand how fragile life was on the vast prairie. They slaughtered wild animals needlessly. They squandered scant resources of wood and water. Some tribes warred against the intruders, but the Americans and their Army continued to come in ever increasing numbers.

In 1849 a cholera epidemic spread from westbound settlers to the tribes. In a short time, half of William Bent's adopted tribe was dead.

When he built his Fort, William Bent couldn't have known what was going to happen in the future, but by the time of this story, he knew the life of the plains and of the plains tribes was being changed forever. And he must have known that he and his Fort were playing a major, if unintended role. Perhaps that was what he was thinking when, on August 21, 1849, he had all the goods and people in the Fort, including his wife, Yellow Woman, and their children, loaded into twenty ox-drawn wagons. The wagons traveled down the Arkansas River and made camp at a site known as "The Big Timbers," then William Bent rode away alone. Later that day, people at the camp heard explosions.

Leon Palladay, a trader from Bent's Fort who was traveling with a government train, also heard the booms. The next day he found the Fort smoldering, the walls crumbled.

No one knows for sure what really happened. Most historians believe William Bent set off the explosions himself. Some think the Fort may have been destroyed by people from one of the tribes.

What do you think happened at Bent's Fort on that day in August 1849?

Bent's Old Fort - Colorado

(From an old sketch by Le Roy Boyd)

Bent's Old Fort National Historic Site in Colorado
Courtesy National Park Service
US Department of Interior

Bent's Fort Today

Bent's Fort is now known as Bent's Old Fort because William Bent built a second fort at The Big Timbers, down the river from where the adobe Fort was destroyed. Bent's New Fort wasn't like a fort at all. It was a simple trading post, built of stone and wood, used *only* for trading. Today a few of those stones still lie on the ground, but over the years, most stones from Bent's New Fort have been used for building houses and barns.

For many years, nothing was left of Bent's Old Fort but a faint outline of raised adobe on the dry prairie. Now the Fort has been reconstructed to look like it did in 1845-46, the happiest time of its history.

You can visit the restored Bent's Old Fort, walk through cool adobe rooms, smell food cooking in the kitchen fireplace, hear the clank of the blacksmith's anvil, and talk with trappers and wagon masters, cooks and carpenters who seem to have escaped from the pages of the past.

Bent's Fort is located seven miles east of La Junta and 13 miles west of Las Animas, Colorado on Highway 194. Communications can be sent to:

Bent's Old Fort National Historic Site
35110 Highway 194 East
La Junta, CO 81050-9523
Phone: (719) 383-5010
http://www.nps.gov/beol

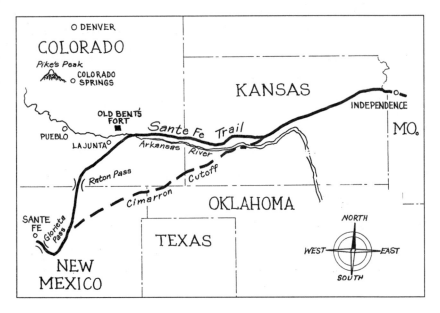

The Santa Fe Trail in 1849 with present-day
state boundaries.

Glossary

adobe: a mixture of mud, water, and a binder such as straw that dries and hardens inside wooden forms to make thick bricks for building.

black soup: the Cheyenne name for coffee.

cholera: a highly infectious, often fatal disease that swept from India through Europe to the United States and to the Native American Tribes of the Great Plains in the mid-1800s.

frijol: the Spanish word for (dry) bean.

fur press: a wooden vise used to compress furs for shipping.

munitions room: a secured room for storing gunpowder and ammunition.

pemmican: a concentrated, high-protein food made by pounding together jerky (dried buffalo meat), fat, and berries.

pox marks: scars from chicken pox and small pox, diseases introduced to Native Americans by immigrants.

tipi: a warm, ventilated, easily assembled shelter made of tall, straight lodgepole pine trunks covered with scraped animal hides.

travois: a carriage of leather and two long poles lashed to a horse to transport provisions, small children, the weak and the sick. The poles are also used as supports for a tipi.

**vision or
vision quest:** a rite of passage from childhood to manhood in which a young Native American male alone in a remote place, gained insight into himself and his future, and returned to his tribe as a brave.

wickiup: a temporary shelter made of branches, often propped against a growing tree.

More Santa Fe Trail Adventure Books
by Mary Peace Finley

- *Soaring Eagle* (ISBN: 1-57168-281-3). The survival adventure story of blond, green-eyed Julio Montoya on the Santa Fe Trail in 1845. Published by Eakin Press (800) 880-8642. RL: 4.0. 1998-99 Colorado Blue Spruce Award nominee.

- *The Teacher's Guide to Soaring Eagle.* Games, activities, puzzles, knowledge links pertaining to the novel and nineteenth century life in the Southwest. Available from the author at www.marypeacefinley.com.

- *White Grizzly* (ISBN: 0-86541-053-4). Available Fall 2000. In this companion novel to *Soaring Eagle*, Julio Montoya's adventure-filled search for identity leads him from Bent's Fort to Independence, Missouri. Published by Filter Press (888) 570-2663. RL: 4.0

Visit the author online!

www.marypeacefinley.com